P9-CSC-287

KEEPERS

BY JERI HANEL WATTS
ILLUSTRATED BY FELICIA MARSHALL

LEE & LOW BOOKS • NEW YORK

Printed in Hong Kong by South China Printing Co. (1988) Ltd.

Book Design by Christy Hale
Book Production by The Kids at Our House

The text is set in Caslon 540.
The illustrations are rendered in acrylic and acrylic oil on watercolor paper.

10 9 8 7 6 5 4 3 2 1
First Edition

Library of Congress Cataloging-in-Publication Data
Watts, Jeri Hanel
Keepers/by Jeri Hanel Watts; illustrated by Felicia Marshall.
p.   cm.
Summary: After Kenyon squanders the money he has saved for his
grandmother's birthday present, he searches for another special gift.
ISBN: 1-880000-58-X
[1. Grandmothers—Fiction. 2. Birthdays—Fiction. 3. Gifts—Fiction.
4. Storytelling—Fiction. 5. Afro-Americans—Fiction.] I. Marshall, Felicia, ill. II. Title.
PZ7.W337Ke 1997
[Fic]—dc21   97-7312
                                                              CIP AC

His grandmother's heavy snoring told Kenyon that she'd finished her storytelling. He liked to listen with his eyes closed, so he hadn't realized she was through until the snore. He loved her stories, as familiar to him as if they had been his own. But he knew she got tired quickly since her stroke, so he rose quietly and eased to the kitchen to glance at the clock.

"Nearly four o'clock," he whispered. He could just make it to the ballfield if he left now. His tired old glove lay in his room, beside the reminder he'd printed in big, bold letters: "90 in two Saturdays." He didn't want to forget a present for his grandmother's ninetieth birthday. Kenyon pounded his cracked glove with his right hand. He didn't have to worry about that yet. He tip-toed to the front door.

"Where you think you're going, boy?"

Kenyon's quiet, easy glide to freedom was frozen by his grandmother's words. "To play baseball," he mumbled.

"Did you finish your homework?" she demanded.

"Mostly finished, Little Dolly." From the corner of his eye, he saw the white hair snap around. Kenyon let the door fall shut and turned as his grandmother lit into him.

"Mostly? Mostly's not good enough, child. There's some things cain't be done mostly. Cain't mostly be dead. You either dead or you not. Cain't be mostly crazy. You either crazy or you not. And—"

"I'll finish," he interrupted. Man, she did take a lot of words to say no.

Little Dolly's voice kept on muttering with her list of non-mostlys, but Kenyon opened his history book and shut out her talking. Since his mother died six years ago he and his dad had lived with Little Dolly. He still didn't know why she was called Little Dolly. There wasn't much little about her. She was a big-boned woman with great big hands and a great big voice and a great lot of words.

Kenyon tried his best to study his history but he couldn't concentrate on all those long-ago dates and names. His mind was filled up with more important things. Things like Mo Davis' fastball and whether he could hit it today like he did yesterday—clean out of the park.

Mo thought he was some kind of pitcher with his real leather glove, but Kenyon didn't mind on days like yesterday, days when Kenyon felt like a hitting machine that could not be denied. That had been a true wallop-bat day.

By the time Kenyon reached the park diamond, he had to take leftovers on team and position.

"It's about time," Mo taunted. "Did you have to help Granny into the sun?"

Kenyon's knuckles burned as he clenched his fists tightly. He didn't like to hear Little Dolly spoken of poorly. So much for another wallop-bat day, he thought.

That evening, Kenyon sat on the peeling floor of the porch, while Little Dolly rested on the swing.

"Tell me a story, Little Dolly," he begged.

"You tell, instead," she answered. "Tell about the stories you read in your history book."

"Aw, those are boring." Kenyon pushed the swing gently. "The only good stories I can tell are about baseball. And you don't care about that."

"That's true enough, I suppose," Little Dolly agreed. "But a good storyteller can make you care with how she weaves the tale. Course, I ain't needing to tell that. Them words are for the next Keeper."

"Keeper?" Kenyon asked.

"Yes, Keeper. Of stories and legends. My grandma said they had Keepers back in Africa for each tribe, but I cain't say about that. Can say we've had Keepers in our family since always. My great grandma, Daisy, my Grandma Dormeen. And me. The Keeper holds onto the past until she can pass it on to the next." Little Dolly squinched her dark brown eyes. "Don't know who I'll hand my tales to, though." Her large fingers plucked at the sleeve of her blouse.

Kenyon stopped the swing and he knelt beside her. "Little Dolly, I'll be the Keeper. I love your stories."

Her eyes looked deep into his, searching.

"Lord, honey, that's nice, but you a boy. I got to find me a girl Keeper. You cain't be a Keeper if you a boy."

The next day Kenyon picked up an old shoe box and carried it to his bed. He slid the top off and dumped the contents onto the quilt. He'd been saving all of his neighborhood-chores money to buy something for Little Dolly's ninetieth birthday. Even if she did drive him crazy about schoolwork, Kenyon thought she was the best. He headed out to see what he could find.

Kenyon went in the bakery first. "Hey, Mrs. Montgomery." The woman behind the counter reached into the glass display case and pulled an oatmeal cookie from the pile. "Oatmeal is good for you in the morning," she said with a wink as she handed the still-warm cookie to Kenyon. "What can I do for you?"

"I'm trying to figure out what to get Little Dolly for her birthday." Kenyon forced his words around the cookie. "One of the things I was considering was one of your strawberry shortcakes. Little Dolly says no one can come close to touching your cake. Would you make one?"

Mrs. Montgomery smiled gently. "If that's what you want. But they're fifteen dollars."

"Oh, I got that and more," he said. "But I'm just looking today."

Kenyon wandered along Main Street, going in and out of shops, talking of ideas for Little Dolly with all of the shopkeepers, for they all knew his grandmother. The antique store, where she could tell stories about many of the items for sale; the carriage ride place, where Little Dolly always delighted the tourists with her tales; the soldier's cemetery, where she and Kenyon helped the caretaker decorate with flags on holidays.

Kenyon was sliding his fingers along the storefronts when he saw, right under his hand, a leather baseball glove. On sale. Real leather.

He went in. He tried it on. It fit as if it had been made just for him. He punched it with his fist and the rich aroma of new leather filled his head. He thought about Mo Davis and within five minutes, that brand spanking-new leather glove slid into a crisp shopping bag.

Kenyon ran to the field and tried it out. Mo wasn't around, but there were plenty of kids to "ooh" and "aah" over his purchase. He fielded grounders with it, spit into it, and scratched his name on it with a penknife.

And then, when he headed home for lunch, streaked with dust and full of pride, then he remembered Little Dolly.

Kenyon felt as if he couldn't breath right. His eyes opened wide and he could feel his heart beating against his ribs the way a bat beats a ball when it connects for a homer.

"What'll I do? What'll I do?"

All the way home, folks asked him if he'd decided yet on the gift for Little Dolly. He managed to mumble something. Mrs. Montgomery looked at that ball glove and he knew she'd figured it out.

When he got asked to a pick-up game later, Kenyon said no and went to his room. His dad came in, feeling all over Kenyon's head, making him stick out his tongue.

"I'm not sick," he told his dad.

"You've never said no to a baseball game, son. Never."

Kenyon slumped onto his bed. "I'm not sick. I'm just stupid."

"Why in the world do you say that?"

"Dad, have you ever done something you were sorry for, but you couldn't change it?" Kenyon looked straight into his father's eyes.

His dad let a breath out slow. "Well, sure. Everybody has, I expect."

"So, what did you do?"

"Told myself I'd do better the next time and then, went on. You can't go back. Can only go forward."

Little Dolly wouldn't be ninety again. He couldn't do better. There wouldn't be a next time.

Shoot, he didn't blame Little Dolly for not trusting him with her stories. He couldn't even be trusted with money and—

The stories. That was it. He *could* give her something.

On Little Dolly's birthday Kenyon and his dad
helped her out to the porch. There were two
presents waiting on the swing.

"Oh my," Little Dolly gushed.

She picked up the smaller present, laughing.
"I know what this is," she said. Every year Dad
got Little Dolly a box of assorted chocolates.
They were her favorites and she always hid
them so she wouldn't have to share. "I'll save
these for later." She tucked the box behind
her arm and reached for the other gift.

As she picked it up, car horns sounded.
"Lord Amighty," Little Dolly said. "What's
happening?"

"Happy Birthday, Miz Bowles!" Shouts came
from the street. And suddenly, the porch spilled
over with people from the town—all of the friends
Little Dolly had made in all her years of living in
Lexington.

Mrs. Montgomery strolled up the walk with
the biggest strawberry shortcake ever. "Happy
Birthday," she said, setting the cake before Little
Dolly. "Make a wish and blow out all these
candles. It isn't every day you turn ninety, you
know." She reached over and hugged Kenyon.

The cake was delicious and everyone had
a good time.

"Don't that beat all," Little Dolly said after everyone had left. "Best birthday I've—" Little Dolly stopped as her foot pushed on Kenyon's present.

"Well, looks like it ain't over yet," she said. "Hand that box up to me, Kenyon."

Little Dolly ripped the paper off as Kenyon shifted from foot to foot. He started apologizing. "It's not much, I know. Not like a carriage ride or a strawberry shortcake . . ."

He stopped when he saw her eyes sparkling. She carefully lifted the gift from the box and delicately touched the handmade book.

"They showed us how to do that at school," Kenyon explained. "How to bind it and all. And inside I put—"

"My stories," she finished. "A book of my stories."

"Yes ma'am."

Little Dolly pulled Kenyon next to her. Tears were spilling over and dancing down her cheeks. "It seems that I was wrong Kenyon," she said. "A Keeper don't have to be a girl. You've done a fine job here, child. Now, I'm going to need to teach you a few things all Keepers got to know. And then, well, you'll need to add some of your own stories. Maybe a few baseball stories, eh?"

Kenyon smiled and slipped his hand into Little Dolly's. It was definitely a wallop-bat day.